D1512291

SCOOBY-DOO'S SUPER GROOVY READER

By Gail Herman

Illustrated by Duendes del Sur

SCHOLASTIC INC.

New York   Toronto   London   Auckland   Sydney
Mexico City   New Delhi   Hong Kong   Buenos Aires

Snack Snatcher, ISBN 0-439-20229-9,
Copyright © 2001 by Hanna-Barbera. Designed by Maria Stasavage.

The Race Car Monster, ISBN 0-439-24236-3,
Copyright © 2001 by Hanna-Barbera. Designed by Maria Stasavage.

The Haunted Ski Lodge, ISBN 0-439-33493-4,
Copyright © 2001 by Hanna-Barbera. Designed by Maria Stasavage.

Mummies at the Mall, ISBN 0-439-34114-0,
Copyright © 2002 by Hanna-Barbera. Designed by Maria Stasavage.

Sea Monster Scare, ISBN 0-439-31831-9,
Copyright © 2002 by Hanna-Barbera.

The Apple Thief, ISBN 0-439-34115-9,
Copyright © 2002 by Hanna-Barbera. Designed by Maria Stasavage.

12 11 10 9 8 7 6 5 4 3 2   6 7 8 9 10/0

Printed in Singapore   46
ISBN 0-681-27924-9
First compilation printing, November 2005

Shaggy, Scooby, and the gang were at the
Coolsville Bake-Off Contest.

"Like, get a noseful of that!" Shaggy sniffed
the air.

"Rmmm-rmmm!" Scooby-Doo sniffed, too.

Scooby and Shaggy had entered the contest.
They were going to bake Scooby Snacks.

"Like, this contest is the best!" Shaggy smiled. "The winner gets free pizza — for a year!" Fred pointed to a booth. "That's your spot," he told Shaggy and Scooby.

Velma, Fred, and Daphne grabbed the supplies.

"These bags weigh a ton!" Velma said.

"What is in here?" asked Daphne.

"Ingredients," said Shaggy. "Flour, sugar . . ."

Then Scooby pulled out a box. "Rizza!"
Scooby cried.

"There's no pizza in Scooby Snacks," Velma
said.

Shaggy took a big cheesy bite. "It's not for
the snacks," he explained. "It's for the
cooks!"

"Rat's right!" said Scooby.

"Humph!" said skinny Ms. Pinchface, in the next booth. "What noisy eating!"
Shaggy and Scooby watched Ms. Pinchface wash lima beans for a veggie pie. Then they spied the Tubb Twins, making double fudge brownies.

Shaggy reached out a hand. Scooby reached out a paw.

"Don't!" said Velma. "You can't eat anybody else's food. It's against the rules. You will be kicked out of the contest."

Daphne smiled. "But *we* can try anything we like!"

"Let's go!" Fred said.

"Like, let's get cooking!" said Shaggy.
Scooby took out more ingredients. Then
they pulled out baking sheets, dough cut-
ters, chef hats, aprons, and finally: another
pizza!

"Whew!" Shaggy yawned. "I'm
tired. If I weren't hungry for
Scooby Snacks, I would take a
nap. Like, let's hurry, Scoob.
So we can snooze!"

Shaggy grabbed the flour. *Splat!* It spilled on the floor. Scooby grabbed the eggs. Crack! They smashed on the table.

"Pour!" Shaggy shouted. "Knead! Mix!"

Finally, the dough was ready.
Shaggy and Scooby shoved the snacks in the
oven. In a flash, they fell asleep.

Across the room, Velma, Fred, and Daphne heard a scream and a thud. It was Ms. Pinchface, a bag of lima beans at her feet.

"What's wrong?" cried Daphne.

"There's a monster!" Ms. Pinchface shouted.

"Over by my table! It's all white and spooky-looking, without any eyes!"

A rumbling noise shook the room.

"I see something on the other side!" Daphne cried.

"Let's go!" said Fred.

17

Velma, Fred, and Daphne ran closer. The noise grew louder. But as they reached the cooking booth, the noise stopped. The monster was gone.

"Like, quiet down, you guys," Shaggy said. "We're sleeping here!"

"We're sorry," said Daphne. "But Ms. Pinchface saw a monster!" Velma added. "A monster?" Shaggy said. "Wake up, Scooby. There's a monster...."

Bing! The oven timer went off.

"Ronster!" Scooby said, and jumped up.

19

"That was the oven," said Velma.
Shaggy opened the oven.
"Zoinks!" cried Shaggy. "It's empty!"
"No Rooby Racks?" said Scooby.

"The monster ate your snacks!" Ms. Pinchface said.

"Like, we didn't see any monster," said Shaggy.

"Of course not," she said. "You were sleeping!"

21

"Look at this!" said Velma.
She pointed to handprints on the oven
door — yellow ones!
"And rook!" cried Scooby. There were
huge paw prints on the floor.
Monster prints!
"Let's look for clues!" said Fred.

"Scooby and Shaggy can guard the oven,"
Velma said.

"Not even for free pizza," Shaggy said.

"Would you do it for Scooby Snacks?" Velma
asked.

Scooby sniffed hungrily. So did Shaggy.

"Rooby Racks? Rokay!"

Velma, Daphne, and Fred followed the trail of paw prints. Shaggy and Scooby were alone.

All at once, they spied a trail of crumbs.

"This could lead to the monster!" said Shaggy.

"Or more Rooby Racks!" said Scooby.

They followed the crumbs.

Scooby licked up one crumb, then another.
"Hey!" said Shaggy. "Leave some for me."
He gobbled some up, too.
Slurp, slurp. They kept their heads to the
ground.

Bump! They crashed into Daphne, Fred, and Velma.

Shaggy rubbed his head. "Like, hey! We're back where we started. And so are you!"

"The crumbs circle the oven, and so do the paw prints," said Velma.

She peeked at Scooby's paws. "White!" she said. She examined Shaggy's hands. "Yellow!" she cried. Fred wiped crumbs from Shaggy's shirt.

"These crumbs are just like the ones on the floor!" he said.

"Shaggy, did you eat the Scooby Snacks?"
"Well, maybe I woke up from my nap for a minute, and ate *some*."
"What about you, Scooby-Doo?" Velma said.
Scooby shrugged. "I rate rome, roo."

"There is no monster!" Velma said. "We saw something white. But it was only Shaggy and Scooby wearing an apron and hat! Shaggy's hands are yellow from egg yolk. He made the handprints! And Scooby's paws are white from flour. He made the paw prints! You both ate the snacks. And you didn't even know it!"

"But we are out of the contest," said Shaggy.
"Now you can try all the food!" said Velma.
Shaggy took a bite of the veggie pie. "Like, this is delicious!" He eyed all the tables.
"And we've only just begun!"
Scooby grinned.
"Scooby Dooby Doo!"

SCOOBY-DOO!

THE RACE CAR MONSTER

"Here's a spot!"

Fred pulled the Mystery Machine into a

parking lot.

"Everybody ready to see car racing?"

35

"It might rain." Velma said. "And there's no roof over the seats." "And no snacks!" Shaggy added. "Ro racks?" said Scooby-Doo. "Ro ray!"

Fred waved a piece of paper. "But I got information in the mail. And free tickets!" Just then a hot dog cart rolled by. Free tickets? Hot dogs?

"Like, what are we waiting for?" said Shaggy.

Suddenly the two buddies
jumped back in the van.
Shaggy's teeth chattered.
Scooby's fur stood on end.

39

"W-w-w-we saw some-thing!" said Shaggy.

"What?" said Velma.

"A riant! Rig, rhite reeth!" said Scooby.

"A giant?" asked Velma. "With big white teeth?"

42

Everyone looked around. But
nothing was there.
"Are you sure about this?"
asked Velma. "Maybe you made
a mistake."

41

"Hot dogs! Get your hot dogs. French fries! Jumbo size!" the hot dog guy called.
Scooby sniffed. "Rummy!"
"Like, maybe we did make a mistake," said Shaggy.

A few minutes later, the gang
sat in their seats.

"Great seats," said Shaggy.

"The first race is about to start," said
Daphne.

A man stood at the starting line. He
waved a flag, and the cars took off.

43

"Wow," said Fred.

"Those drivers really go!"

The cars raced around the track, then passed the gang again.

"Check out those squealing tires!" said Shaggy.

"Rokay," said Scooby.

He leaned over the railing.

"Not so far, good buddy," Shaggy said.

All of a sudden, an engine backfired. Shaggy and Scooby jumped in fright — right over the railing!

Thud! They fell onto a speeding car.

"Hang on!" cried Shaggy.

"Ruh-roh," Scooby cried.

There it was again. White flashing teeth. Big bloodshot eyes. It *was* a monster!

The car zoomed past.

Rrrrrr! The monster roared.

Frightened, Shaggy and Scooby shot up in the air.

Thud! They dropped back into their seats.

"Stop clowning around," Fred
said. "I'm trying to watch the race."
"Ronster!" cried Scooby.
"We saw that thing again," Shaggy gasped.
"And it really is a monster!"

"Sure, guys," said Fred. He was watching the race. "Whatever you say."

"Did you hear us, Velma? Daphne?"

"Go, cars, go!" they shouted, excited.

Scooby and Shaggy slumped in their seats. Nobody was listening.

Then the race was over.

"Did you say something?" said Velma.

"We saw the monster again!" Shaggy cried.

"Why didn't you say so?" said Fred. "Let's investigate!"

Velma nodded. "Let's start in the parking lot. That's where Shaggy and Scooby saw the monster."

"I'm not going near that parking lot," said Shaggy.

"Re either," Scooby said.

"Come on, guys," said Fred.

Shaggy and Scooby shook their heads.

"Please?" said Daphne.

They shook their heads harder.

"We have Scooby Snacks in the van," said Velma. "And the van is in the parking lot."

Everyone hurried to the van. Velma started throwing things out of the back.

"I have those Snacks somewhere," said Velma.

All at once, a roar thundered through the lot.

Everyone tumbled into the van. *Crunch!* Scooby landed on the Scooby Snacks.

"Yum! Scooby crumbs!" said Shaggy, digging in.

RRRRRR! The monster reared up
in front of the gang.
"Zoinks!" cried Shaggy.
It stood as high as the treetops.
Sharp teeth flashed.

"Let's get out of here!"

The Mystery Machine took off. But the
monster was right behind . . . chasing
them . . . getting closer!

All at once, more monsters appeared.
Dozens of monsters. All different colors.
All different shapes.

"I'm driving onto the racetrack," Fred cried. "It's the only place to go!" Velma saw the stands. People were cheering. Jinkies, she thought, that's strange.

Then she had an idea. She grabbed the information about the racetrack.

"Like, now you're reading?" said Shaggy. "When there are monsters chasing us?"

"They're monsters all right," said Velma. "Monster trucks!"

Velma showed everyone the racing schedule.
"Second race: Monster trucks."
Just then they crossed the finish line.
Fred braked. Everyone got out of the van.
"See?" said Velma. "Those trucks are made up to look like monsters. Teeth and all!"

A man came up to them, holding a trophy.
"Congratulations!" he said.
"Re ron!" said Scooby.
"Like, cool!" said Shaggy. "And we weren't even trying!"
"Scooby-Dooby-Doo!"

SCOOBY-DOO!

THE HAUNTED SKI LODGE

"Rrrrr!" "Brrrr!" Scooby-Doo and Shaggy
hugged each other to keep warm.

"Like, it's freezing out here," said Shaggy.

"Well, it is winter," said Velma.

"And we are outside, waiting to ski," Daphne
added.

"And you are eating ice cream," said Fred.

Shaggy grinned. "Well, Scoob, old buddy.
Let's get some *hot* dogs then!"
Scooby's teeth chattered. "Rummy!"
"Ski lodge, here we come!" said Shaggy.

"Not so fast!" said Fred. "We came to
this mountain to ski. And that is what
we are going to do."

"But we better do it fast," Velma said. "I heard there is a storm watch. If the snow gets bad, the mountain may close."

Velma, Fred, and Daphne hopped onto
the ski lift.

"See you at the top!" said Daphne.

Then it was Shaggy and Scooby's turn.

"Oomph!" The bench crashed into them, and
they tumbled onto the seat.
"Going up!" said Shaggy.
The buddies glided over the trees to the top
of the mountain.

"Time to get off, good buddy," Shaggy said.
"Count to three, then we jump."
"Rokay," said Scooby. "Ron, roo . . ."

"Ree!" Scooby and Shaggy jumped off the ski lift. "Wooooaaaaah!"
They slipped and slid and teetered and tottered off the path, and away from their friends. They couldn't stop.

Finally, they stumbled to a stop — in front
of another ski lodge.

"How about a rest?" said Shaggy.

"Reah!" said Scooby.

Shaggy grinned. "Groovy. We can get those
hot dogs now!"

Inside, the lodge was dark. Cobwebs hung from the ceiling. Sheets covered tables. And dust covered everything.

"There's no one here," said Shaggy,
disappointed. "No cooks or waiters."
He picked up a phone. "And no dial tone.
We can't even call for pizza."

"Rait!"

Scooby padded through swinging doors, into the kitchen.

He sniffed around the cabinets.

"Rummy!"

"Yummy?" said Shaggy. He opened a door.
Out tumbled popcorn, potato chips, and all
sorts of food and drinks.
"Eat first!" Shaggy shouted. "Ski later!"

79

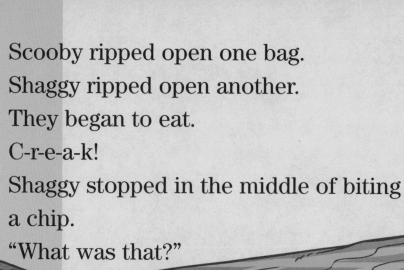

Scooby ripped open one bag.
Shaggy ripped open another.
They began to eat.
C-r-e-a-k!
Shaggy stopped in the middle of biting
a chip.
"What was that?"

C-R-E-A-K!
Slowly, slowly, the kitchen door swung open.
Slowly, slowly, the kitchen door swung closed.
"Whoooo!"
A ghostly cry filled the air.

Boom! Something crashed upstairs. Shaggy
dropped his popcorn. Scooby dropped his
chips.

"Rhost!" shouted Scooby.

"Ghost!" shouted Shaggy.

Shapes swirled outside the windows.
Bangs echoed through the lodge.
"Whoooo! Whoooo!"
"Like, it's not just one ghost!" Shaggy
moaned. "This place is crawling with ghosts!"

They ran for the door.

"Push!" said Shaggy. Scooby pushed. But the door wouldn't open.

"Rull!" Scooby said. Shaggy pulled. But the door still wouldn't open.

"We're trapped!" Shaggy cried.

They crawled under the table.

"Oh, why did we go off on our own?" Shaggy sobbed. "How are we going to get out?"

All at once, the door swung open. Great
white shapes floated inside.
"Zoinks! They're closing in!" said Shaggy.
One lifted an arm and pointed right at them.
"Raggy!" shouted Scooby. "Run!"

The buddies raced around the ghosts.

"Stop!" one commanded.

Shaggy skidded to a stop. The voice sounded familiar.

"What are you guys doing?" asked another ghost.

"Are you okay?" asked the third.

"Velma?" said Shaggy. "Fred?"
"Raphne?" Scooby added.
Velma, Daphne, and Fred shook off the snow
covering their heads, arms, and legs.

"Of course it's us," said Fred. "We followed your tracks to find you."
"We thought you were ghosts," Shaggy explained, "and that this place is haunted."

Whooooo! Whoooo! Boom! Crash!

Shaggy jumped into Scooby's arms.

"See?" said Shaggy. "Listen to that!"

"The wind is making the whooo noise,"
Velma said.

"And the booms?" asked Shaggy.

"That's just tree branches hitting the roof."
Shaggy pointed to the white shapes outside
the window. "Explain that!"
Fred laughed. "Easy. It's snow blowing
around."

"But the door opened and closed by itself," said Shaggy. "Then it was stuck. This place really is haunted!"

Shaggy tried to run but slipped in a puddle of melted snow.

"Don't be silly," said Velma. "The wind blew against the door so hard, it wouldn't open."

Daphne patted Scooby. "The storm is really bad. The mountain is closing."
Fred checked his watch. "We missed the last ski lift run. What are we going to do now?"

Velma shrugged. "We can build a fire and wait right here."

Scooby gulped. "Rere?"

"This place gives me the creeps, but okay," Shaggy said, and he walked away.

"Raggy!" shouted Scooby.

"Like, cool it, good buddy," said Shaggy. He pointed to the fire. "I'm just getting the marshmallows!"

"See, guys, this ski lodge isn't so bad," said
Velma.
"So long as we don't run out of marshmallows
it's cool. Right, Scooby?" Shaggy replied.
"Scooby-Dooby-Doo!"

CARTOON NETWORK®

SCOOBY-DOO!

MUMMIES AT THE MALL

The Coolsville Mall was packed. Scooby-Doo, Shaggy, and the gang stood in a crowd of people.

"Let's figure out what we want to do," said Shaggy, "before we get squeezed any tighter."

All at once, the crowd moved through a set of doors.

"Oh!" said Daphne. "We're in front of the movie theater."

"The movie must be about to start," said Velma.

Fred nodded. "We should go!"

Shaggy pointed to the movie poster.
"*Mummies on the Loose* is playing."
He shivered. "Like, we'll catch you
later. Scoob and I will find something
else to do."

Shaggy and Scooby stopped in a pet store.

Two dogs were being groomed.

"Care for a day of beauty?" Shaggy asked Scooby.

Scooby shook his head. "Ro way!"

Next they went to a store called Snooze City. Shaggy and Scooby gazed at the cozy beds, soft pillows, and thick blankets. Scooby yawned. Shaggy stretched. "Forty winks sounds pretty good to me. What do you think, good buddy?"

"Good buddy?" Shaggy whirled around. Scooby wasn't there! Then Shaggy spotted him. He had run outside. He was seated in front of a giant hot dog.

"Hey, that's just a guy in costume," said Shaggy. The hot dog guy handed Shaggy a flyer.

"'All-You-Can-Eat Day at Coolsville Mall,'" Shaggy read. "'Go to any restaurant! EAT till you're stuffed! All for one price!'"

"First stop, Big Burger!" Shaggy shouted, leading Scooby into a restaurant. The hours passed, burger by burger.

Finally, Scooby and Shaggy came out. Scooby patted his belly. "Had enough?" Shaggy asked. "Well, just in case, I stashed some burgers in my pockets."

BIG BURGER

Next came Hot Dog Hut, then Sausage
Shack. Each time it was the same.
The friends stuffed themselves. Then
Shaggy stuffed his pockets!

Finally, they waddled out of the Barbecue Pit. "That mummy movie will be over soon," Shaggy said to Scooby. "Let's go meet the gang."

All at once, shouts rang through the mall. Heavy footsteps echoed all around. *Thud, thud.*

THUD! They grew louder and louder. Scooby's ears quivered.

"Hey, relax, good buddy." Shaggy laughed.
"Look — it's just the hot dog guy!"
But something was behind him. *Two*
somethings! Wrapped in bandages!
"Rummies!" yelled Scooby.
"Mummies!" yelled Shaggy.

"The mummies are chasing the hot dog guy," Shaggy said. "So we should be safe." But the hot dog guy had disappeared. Now the mummies were after *them*.

"Zoinks!" yelled Shaggy. "Run!"

The chase was on . . . past the restaurants . . . past Snooze City. There were pillows everywhere. "The mummies must have torn this place up!" said Shaggy.

They raced past the pet store.
The mummies had struck
there, too!

Shaggy pointed to a sports store. "Let's hide in there!" The buddies ran inside. They twisted around to check for the mummies. *CRASH!* They slammed into a huge pile of tennis balls.

Balls rolled everywhere. Shaggy and Scooby couldn't run. They couldn't even stand.

The mummies were coming closer! Finally, Shaggy and Scooby grabbed tennis rackets.

"Service!" shouted Shaggy as they swung at balls and cleared a path. "Now let's go!"

"Quick!" Shaggy called to Scooby. "In here!" They raced into Coolsville Clothes. They slipped into big coats and floppy hats. "Great disguise!" said Shaggy. "The mummies will never find us now!"

Thud, thud! "Rikes!" Scooby cried. The mummies were smarter than they thought. They were coming toward them!

Shaggy and Scooby sped out the door.

"There's the gang!" said Shaggy.

Scooby jumped into Daphne's arms.

"Excuse me, sir," said Daphne.

"Can I help you?"

"You can help *us*!" said Shaggy. He and
Scooby whipped off their disguises.

"What's going on?" asked Fred.

In a flash, Shaggy explained about the mummies. How they made a mess at the pet store and Snooze City. How they chased the hot dog guy, and now were chasing them.

"Hmmmm," said Velma, thinking it over.

Then Fred wrinkled his nose. "What's that smell?"

Shaggy pulled out hamburgers and hot dogs from his pockets. "Leftovers!"

Just then a pet store worker ran over. "Have you seen King and Queen?" he asked. "Two of our dogs disappeared."

"Oh, no!" wailed Shaggy.
"The mummies got them!"
Thud, thud!
"And here they come —
for us!"

Velma stepped in between Shaggy, Scooby, and the mummies. She held up her hand. "Stay!"

The mummies stopped.

"Wow," said Shaggy. "Those mummies are good listeners!"

"They're not mummies," Velma said. "They're King and Queen, and I think they're hungry. They must have thought the hot dog guy was a real hot dog, and the two of you smell like . . . well . . ." She pointed to the food. "Like lunch."

"But they sure look like mummies," Shaggy said.

Velma pulled off the bandages. "These are sheets. They must have run into Snooze City and gotten wrapped up while they were making a mess."

"Poor things," said Daphne.

Shaggy looked at Scooby and shrugged. Then he gave the dogs all the food. "There goes our snack." He sighed. "But I'm not afraid of mummies anymore!"

"Hey, Scoob. How about we get some popcorn?"
"Scooby-Dooby-Doo!"

CARTOON NETWORK®

SCOOBY-DOO!

SEA MONSTER SCARE

It was a perfect day for the beach.
"Ret's ro!" Scooby-Doo said to his friends.
"Scoob is right," Shaggy said. "Surf's up!"

Velma pulled a wagon. It was filled with shovels and pails and flags. "I'm ready to make a one-of-a-kind sand castle!" she said.

Scooby pulled another wagon. It was
filled with sandwiches and pizza, hot
dogs, and tons of chips.
"We're ready for a one-of-a-kind lunch!"
Shaggy said.

"This is a good spot!" said Velma. She took everything from the wagon. Then she filled the pails with sand. Fred turned them over. And Daphne lifted them up.

"This sand castle will be perfect!" said Velma.

"Mmm-mmm! This sandwich is perfect," said Shaggy.

Scooby and Shaggy ate their way through piles of food. Finally, they burped.

"Like, we're all done!" said Shaggy.

"Us too," said Velma.

Shaggy and Scooby looked over. Their
jaws dropped. "Holy cow!" said Shaggy.
The castle had moats and bridges, and
winding steps. Flags flew from towers.
"It is good," Velma agreed.
"Like, I'm not talking about the castle,"
said Shaggy. "We're out of food!"

"Out of food?" Daphne laughed.

"And we didn't have a bite!" said Fred.

Scooby hung his head. "Rorry."

"Sorry," Shaggy echoed. "How about Scoob and I make a food run? There's a Snack Shack down the beach!"

Scooby and Shaggy set off. A little while later, they were back. At least, they thought they were.

They saw the blanket. They saw Velma's book. But that was all.

"Zoinks!" said Shaggy. "Everyone has disappeared! And so has the sand castle!"

All around them, people snatched up blankets. They threw books, bottles of sunscreen, and other things into beach bags. They rushed away.

"Something horrible has happened!" cried Shaggy. "We need clues!"

Scooby gazed out to sea. "Rook!" he gasped.
A giant sea serpent rode the waves.
"Like, that thing did it!" said Shaggy. "It took
the sand castle, *and* the gang!"

Shouts rang out across the water.
"It's getting closer!" Shaggy cried.
Scooby yelped, "Run, Raggy!"

The buddies took off. They jumped over people. They scooted around umbrellas. But the sea serpent was close behind.
It was coming onto the beach!

"A surfboard, Scoob!" Shaggy shouted. "Quick! Hop on!"

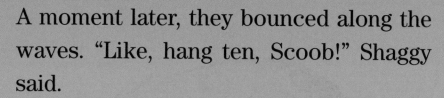

A moment later, they bounced along the waves. "Like, hang ten, Scoob!" Shaggy said.

But they couldn't surf fast enough. The monster was closing in!

The sea grew rough. Scooby and Shaggy hung on. Wave after wave. Up, down. Up, down.

Scooby turned green. "Don't lose
your lunch, good buddy," Shaggy said.
Up, down. Up, down.
Shaggy turned green too.

All at once, a giant wave crashed over them. Shaggy clung to Scooby. Scooby clung to Shaggy.
Whoosh!

151

Up, up, up they went. The surfboard
went one way. Scooby and Shaggy
went the other way.

They hung in the air. Then they dropped —
fast. Right onto the back of the sea serpent!

"Help!" "Relp!" they cried.
"Don't worry," said Velma. "We're
right here."
Scooby spun around. Velma,
Fred, and Daphne were on the
serpent's back, too.

"We've got to get off!"
Shaggy screamed.
"Relax," said Fred.
"The ride will be over
soon."

"Ride?" said Shaggy. "The serpent gives rides?"
"It's not a real monster," said Daphne. "It's a float."
Scooby and Shaggy gazed around. People were laughing and having fun.

"But what about the people on the beach?"
asked Shaggy. "Why did they run away? And
what about the sand castle? I thought a monster wiped it out."

"The sand castle is gone?" Velma gasped.

Then she sighed. "It must have been the tide. That's what happens with sand castles. The tide sweeps them away. And those people? They were only moving away from the water."

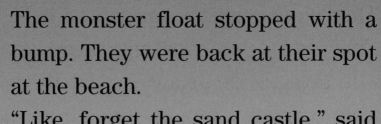

The monster float stopped with a bump. They were back at their spot at the beach.

"Like, forget the sand castle," said Shaggy. "All our food has been swept away, too!"

"Rack Rack?" said Scooby.

"Snack Shack!" agreed Shaggy.

Scooby-dooby-doo!

CARTOON NETWORK®

SCOOBY-DOO!

THE APPLE THIEF

Scooby-Doo and Shaggy jumped out
of the Mystery Machine.
"Like, any pizza around here?" said
Shaggy. "I'm starving."
"Rizza! Rizza!" Scooby said.

The rest of the gang climbed out of the van.
Velma laughed. "There's no pizza here."

"This is an apple orchard," Fred added.

"That's right," said Daphne. "We're here to
pick apples."

"We're here to *pick* apples?" Shaggy
moaned. "Not eat them?"
"That comes later," Daphne promised.

"Like, I'm so hungry," Shaggy said. "I'm going to pick more apples than anyone!"

"Don't be so sure." Velma smiled. "I've read books about picking apples. I know exactly how to do it."

Shaggy looked at her. He was much taller than Velma was. He could reach more apples.

"Let's have a contest," he said. "We can split into groups. And the winners get to eat all the apples!"

"I don't know," said Velma. "This is a big place. Maybe we should stay together. So we don't get lost."

Shaggy pictured apple pies and apple jam. Scooby pictured candy apples and sweet applesauce. "Ro way!" said Scooby.

"Then let the contest begin!" said Velma. Everyone took baskets. Shaggy and Scooby went one way. Daphne led Fred and Velma the other way.

Shaggy reached for apples way up high.
Scooby bent for apples way down low.
One by one, they put them in the basket.

A little later, Shaggy checked the basket. "Zoinks!" he cried. "It's empty!"

Shaggy eyed Scooby. "Did you eat the apples?"

"Ro ray," said Scooby. "Rou ate the rapples!"

"Like, no way for me, too!" Shaggy said.

They both shrugged. "Let's start over," said Shaggy.

They reached and pulled and picked and tossed. Shaggy peeked in the basket. Empty again!

"Scooby, stop eating the apples!" Shaggy cried.

Scooby shook his head. "Rou rop eating!"

"*You're* not eating the apples," said Shaggy. "And *I'm* not eating the apples. So who's eating the apples?"

All at once, Scooby shivered. It was getting
cold. The sun was going down.
They needed apples to win the contest. But
the apples kept disappearing!
"We have to figure this out," said Shaggy.
"Before it is too late."

"Who did this?" Shaggy called out.

"Who?" A voice called back.

Shaggy and Scooby jumped. Someone was teasing them. But they couldn't see anybody.

"We should call the police!" said Shaggy.

"*Call!*" said a voice.

They peered into the darkness. Still no one.

"Someone is out there," Shaggy said.
"But we can't see him. He must be
invisible!"

All of a sudden, an apple hit Shaggy
on the head.

"Ouch!"

An apple hit Scooby on the head.

"Rouch!"

"It's an apple attack!" Shaggy cried. Apples crashed down, one after the other. "Run for your life, Scoob old buddy," Shaggy said.

They turned to speed
away. But they slipped on
wet leaves.

Crash! They bumped into
something . . . big . . . tall . . .
Giant arms trapped them.
"It's the invisible man!" Shaggy
shouted.
They tumbled to the ground in a heap.

Boom! Boom! They heard thudding footsteps. Breaking branches.
But they couldn't see a thing. More invisible people!
"It's a whole army!" Shaggy wailed. "We're goners!"

"Jinkies!" said a voice. "We finally found you!"

"The invisible man sounds just like Velma!" said Shaggy.

Velma pulled a wet leaf from Shaggy's eyes. "It *is* Velma," she said.

"What?" Shaggy leaped to his feet.
"You're all here! You must have scared
away the invisible men."

Shaggy explained about the missing
apples. The voices teasing them. The
apples hitting them on the head. The
giant arms grabbing them.

185

Velma pushed away two branches. "These are your giant arms. You ran into a tree. But you couldn't tell because leaves covered your eyes."

"*Who! Call!*" the voices said again.

"Hmm," said Velma. "That 'whoooo' sounds like a hoot. And the 'call'? That sounds like *caw*."

"An owl and a crow!" Daphne exclaimed.

Next, Velma picked up the basket. "Aha! There's a hole in it! That's why the apples disappeared. They kept falling out!"

"But what about the apple attack?" Shaggy asked as another apple hit his head. "Ouch!"
Fred grinned. "The apples are ripe."
"That's right," Velma agreed. "The wind blows them down. Or they fall on their own."

The mystery was solved. But now it was so dark, the gang could hardly see.

"How will we find our way back?" asked Daphne.

"Look at this, Scoob!" said Shaggy. "All our apples! In a row!"

"It's like a trail," said Velma. "We can follow the apples to find our way back."

"But," said Shaggy, "how do we know who won the contest?" Velma grinned. "You can walk, eat, and count at the same time." "One." *Crunch.* "Two." *Crunch.* "Scooby-dooby-doo!"